Cami Kangaroo and Wyatt Too

Cami Kangaroo
Has Too Much Stuff!

written by Stacy C. Bauer • illustrated by Rebecca Sinclair

RODNEY K
PRESS

Cami Kangaroo Has Too Much Stuff!
Cami Kangaroo and Wyatt Too
Published by Rodney K Press
www.rodneykpress.com
info@rodneykpress.com
Minneapolis, MN

Library of Congress Control Number: 2019938287
Bauer, Stacy Author
Sinclair, Rebecca Illustrator
Cami Kangaroo Has Too Much Stuff!

ISBN: 978-0-9998141-1-6

JUVENILE FICTION

All inquires of this book can be sent to the author.
For more information or to book an event, please visit www.stacycbauer.com

For my parents, who have always been there for me
and taught me that love is the most important
"stuff" in life.
-S.C.B.

For my family and friends who have helped me get
through life's clutter. Thank you for all your support!
-R.S.

It was lunch time at the Kangaroo house. Taking another bite of her salad, Cami thought about how much fun she was going to have at her cousin Savannah's party later that day.

"Your room needs to be clean before we head to Savannah's party, Cami," Daddy Kangaroo reminded her.

"Okay," Cami sighed. She was not excited to clean her room.

Cami's room was full of treasures:
rocks, shells, feathers,
toys...Cami loved them all.

She loved collecting them,

Sorting them,

and building
with them.

Cami peeked inside her pouch. She pulled out a brown button that had fallen off her sweater, a copper coin from Daddy, and a chipped blue block she had found in the yard.

"Hmm," Cami said. "What should I make with these?"
Her mind overflowed with ideas.

"How's it going, Cami?" Mommy called up the stairs.
"Is your room clean yet? We have to leave at 1:00 if we're going to be on time for the party!"

Cami groaned and started cleaning.

What could that be?

Ding!
Ding!
Ding!

"My favorite bell!" Cami put the bell inside her pouch and slowly continued cleaning.

Suddenly she gasped. Savannah had asked her to give back her stuffed puppy; she had to find it!

She picked up the bucket of shells. Maybe Savannah's puppy was in there.

Cami dumped the shells out. *Nope.*

But she did find two pretty pink shells that were quickly added to her pouch.

Maybe the puppy was in the closet.

Cami tugged at the door,
but it didn't budge.

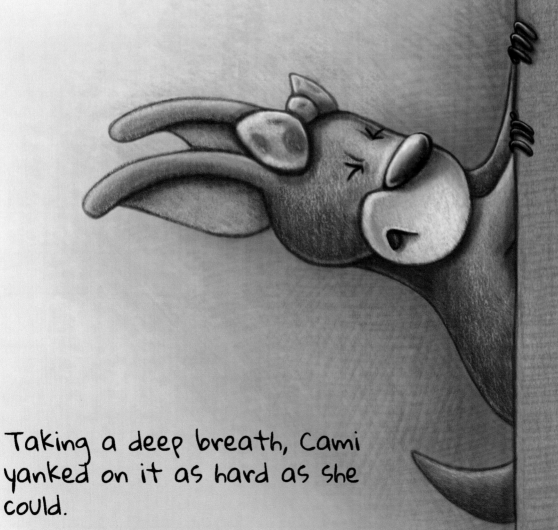

Taking a deep breath, Cami
yanked on it as hard as she
could.

"Ugh…" she groaned. "Oof!" She kicked out her legs and clambered to her feet.

"I have to clean my room and find that puppy!" she thought with a frown.

As she hopped toward a pile of blankets, Cami heard a muffled giggle coming from beneath it. She began digging.

Suddenly, her brother popped out!

"Wyatt!" Cami exclaimed, pulling him from the heap of blankets.

Cami was showing Wyatt some of her favorite rocks when she heard the door open. She quickly slipped the rocks into her pouch.

"It's time to go!" Daddy shoved the door open and hopped inside. He looked around the room with a frown. "Cami, your room is even messier than before!"

"I know! But Daddy, I've lost Savannah's puppy!" Cami cried.

"Well, what do you think we could do to find it quickly so we're not late to the party?" Daddy asked.

"Clean my room?" Cami replied, feeling badly that she hadn't done it already.

"Cleaning your room can be overwhelming," Daddy said. "Let's do one thing at a time."

Together, Cami and Daddy made her bed and put her hair bows into a dresser drawer.

Wyatt put Cami's books on the bookshelf and her dolls in their bin.

As Cami was putting feathers into a little bowl on her desk, she spied something sticking out of a drawer.

"Look what I found!" she said triumphantly.

"Whew! You must be so happy," Daddy smiled.

"I don't like losing things," Cami admitted. "Especially when they belong to someone else. Keeping my room clean will help me keep track of things."

Cami was proud. She had found Savannah's puppy and her room was finally clean!

"Is everyone ready to go? We're going to be late!" Mommy called.

"Yes! I cleaned my room *and* found Savannah's puppy!" Cami stopped and rummaged around inside of her pouch to show Mommy. *Oh no!* She began to empty her pouch out onto the yard.

"Not again!" she cried. "I don't want to miss the party!"

"Didn't you *just* have it?" Daddy asked. Cami felt around inside her pouch again.

"Got it!" she exclaimed with relief.

"Great! Let's go!" Mommy said.

As they hopped to the car, Daddy tripped over some tools in the garage.

Cami chuckled, "Daddy, maybe both of us need to keep our things more organized!"

"You're right about that, Cami!" Daddy Kangaroo laughed.

"I think it's safe to say this whole family has *too* much stuff!" Mommy said. "Tomorrow, we'll spend some time organizing. Now let's get to that party!"

About the Author

Born and raised in a suburb of Minneapolis, MN, Stacy C. Bauer is a wife, teacher and mother of two. She has been writing since she was a child and loves sharing stories of her kids' antics and making people laugh. Her first book, *Cami Kangaroo Has Too Many Sweets!* was published in May 2018 and is available on Amazon.

You can find out more about Stacy and her books at www.stacycbauer.com

About the Illustrator

Rebecca Sinclair has enjoyed drawing pictures since early childhood. She received her MFA in children's book illustration from the Academy of Art University in San Francisco.

Rebecca has illustrated three children's books, including two from the *Cami Kangaroo and Wyatt Too* series. You can find Rebecca illustrating in Grand Rapids, MI with her french bulldog, Phoebe.

To view more of Rebecca's work, visit her website at www.rebeccasinclairstudio.com

Real Parent's Advice On How To Help Your Child Keep His/Her Room Organized:

"Talk with your child about how they think their room should be organized. Use clear bins so they can see what is in each one."
-Anna H, IL

"Put pictures along with words on bins so kids can see and read where their toys are supposed to go."
-Jakki T, MN

"Box up half of the items and store out of sight! Organize remaining items and let the child enjoy what they have in their room for the next 3 months, then switch up the items."
-Sandi H, MD

"Provide storage bins and remind her that the bins are there to help her. Let her take responsibility for her messy room."
-Jessica S, Quebec

"Sweep everything to the center of the room, set a 20 minute timer, and tell them that whatever is left when the timer goes off gets donated."
-Kimberly P, MO

"Let your child display their creations until recycling/garbage day, then they have to go."
-Correna C, Ontario, CA

"Create a checklist of what needs to be picked up before bed each night."
-Kristen B, GA